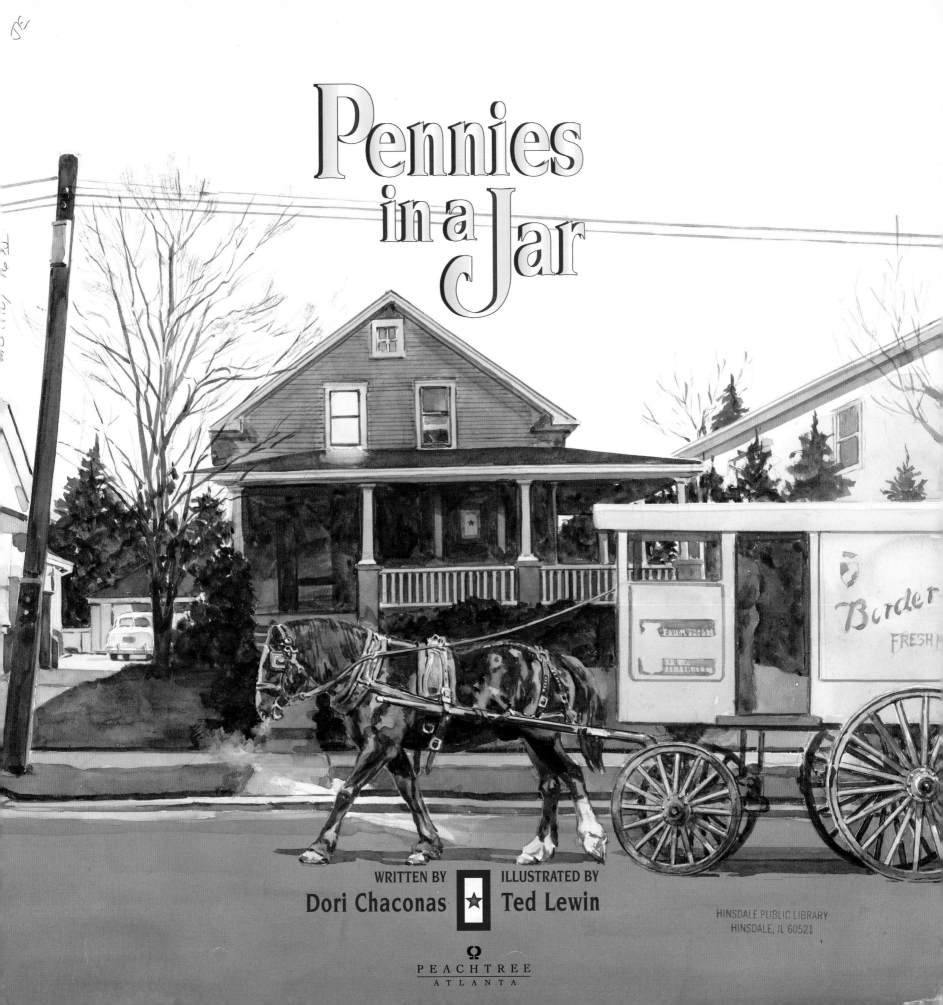

Pennies
in a Jar

WRITTEN BY
Dori Chaconas

ILLUSTRATED BY
Ted Lewin

Ω
PEACHTREE
ATLANTA

The day Dad went away to the war, I cried. He hugged me and told me to be brave.

But I was afraid of so many things.

Like how Mom and I had to take care of things by ourselves now.

And the loud noises in our neighborhood when they tested the air raid sirens.

And thinking about Dad listening to bombs and guns.

I was even afraid of everyday things. Especially the street horses.

We used to sit on the front porch steps, me and Dad. Now I sat there by myself and counted the pennies in my green glass jar. Dad's birthday was coming up. I was saving to buy him a present. Something special—just from me. Mom said she would mail my present overseas with the socks she was knitting.

I heard the ragman holler out from a block away.

Lickety-split, I tore into the house and grabbed the bundle of newspapers from the pantry. Then I slammed back through the screen door—*BANG!*—and grunted the newspapers out to the curb.

A street horse named Josephina was pulling the rag wagon down our street. The ragman sat high on a wooden seat.

"Rags!" *Clop-ta-clop.* "Newspapers! Rags!" *Clop-ta-clop.*

"Whoa-up!" the ragman called when he saw my bundle of papers. He dropped a heavy iron disk on the pavement— *THONCK*—so that Josephina wouldn't walk off. It looked like the horse-stopper was the anchor and Josephina was the ship.

The heavy smell of horse filled up my nose and mouth. Josephina swung her head around and looked straight at me. Her teeth were as big as piano keys.

I jumped back. Had Josephina ever bitten anyone?

My dad got bitten by a horse once, when he was a kid. He had a moon-shaped scar on his shoulder. "Horses are like people, son," he said. "Sometimes you meet a real stinker, but most of them are good."

The ragman threw my newspapers into the back of the wagon.

"Every bit helps," he said, "for the war effort. Got any scrap iron? It's good for building ships and airplanes."

I thought about the iron horseshoe over our back door. Dad nailed it up there to look like a U.

"That way it will catch good luck and hold it in," Dad said. "If you hang it upside down, all the good luck might fall out."

It wasn't a good idea to sell a lucky horseshoe. I wouldn't want any bad luck to keep my dad from coming home from the war.

"Only the newspapers," I told the ragman, keeping my eye on his horse. She gave a loud snort, ready to move on.

"You want to feed her a carrot?" the ragman asked.

I took a step back and shook my head. "Not today," I said.

The man shrugged. "Well, maybe next time."

I went back to the front porch and counted my pennies all over again, dropping them back into my green glass jar.

Pleek! Pleek! Pleek! Fifty-six!

Tuesdays and Fridays were milk days. Mr. Lacey was our milkman. His street horse was named Nell.

"Good morning to you," Mr. Lacey called out when Nell stopped in front of our house.

I watched Mr. Lacey line up three bottles of milk on our porch. He put our three empty bottles into his wire basket.

"Can I carry those for you, Mr. Lacey?" I asked.

Chink-a-chink-a-chink. The bottles and basket bumped against my leg.

When Nell saw Mr. Lacey, she nickered and threw her head up and down. She stamped her foot.

I made a fast stop at the edge of the sidewalk.

"My dad's not afraid of horses," I blurted out. "He grew up on a farm."

Mr. Lacey looked at me kind of funny. Then he nodded and gave me a penny for helping. Nell was already moving to the next house.

Dad said that after he got bitten, he never wanted to go near a horse again. But Grandpa needed him to help with the chores.

"If something is important enough, you just have to do it," Dad told me. "Even if you're scared."

O nce a week, the garbage wagon came by. It was pulled by Billy and Bailey— the biggest street horses of all. They had feet as big and heavy as buckets filled with iron.

"Whoa!" Albert called, holding the reins. Two other men carried canvas baskets on their shoulders to collect the garbage. They scooped it up and dumped it into the open wagon.

"If my dad was here, he could drive that team," I called to Albert. "He used to drive my grandpa's hay wagon. I rode on the back of it once."

"Want to ride in the back of this wagon?" Albert asked, chuckling.

I held my nose and shook my head. On a hot summer day, the garbage wagon smelled worse than an army of skunks.

"No, thanks."

Albert just laughed again.

Billy and Bailey suddenly shook themselves. Their traces and braces jangled and jumped. I jumped, too, and ran back to the porch. I was glad when the garbage wagon was gone.

That afternoon, I sat on the porch step writing a letter. "Dad, I wish you could come home," I began. "If you were here…"

I closed my eyes and thought about a hundred things I wanted to tell my dad. But I didn't know how to sort them all out.

A soft snort made me open my eyes. On the sidewalk right in front of my house stood a man with a pony. The pony had a saddle on his back. His mane and tail shimmered in the sun.

"Hey, kid," the man called out. "You want to ride this here pony?"

"Me?" I asked.

A large camera hung around the man's neck. "I'll take a picture of you on the pony," he said. "Only fifty cents."

I didn't want to tell the man I was afraid.

"What's the pony's name?" I asked.

"His name is Freedom."

"Freedom," I whispered. Dad went away to the war to fight for freedom. Dad would like that name.

"If my dad were here…" I started to say. But my dad *wasn't* here.

I shook my head. "No thanks, mister."

I watched the man and his pony walk away. A sadness as big as a melon filled up the inside of me. What would Dad think if he saw me now?

And then I remembered what he had said. If something is important enough, you just have to do it.

That was when I knew exactly what kind of special birthday present I wanted to buy for Dad with the pennies in my green glass jar. And I knew it was something important.

"Hey, mister!" I shouted. "Hey, mister, come back!"

I ran down the sidewalk after him, my heart pounding. "I do want my picture taken with Freedom!"

The photographer stopped and opened his canvas bag. He pulled out a soft leather vest trimmed with fringes. He slipped it on me, and I felt its weight against my shoulders and back. Then he plopped a real cowboy hat on my head. It looked real, anyway.

My knees felt like noodles. But I tried as hard as I could to be brave.

The man helped me into the saddle. It was slippery smooth. I started to slide and my heart punched against my ribs. I was going to fall off this horse!

"Hold on with your knees, kid," the photographer said. I squeezed them tight as he began leading Freedom back toward my house. I swayed back and forth in the saddle, but I didn't slip again.

I was riding a horse! It was a small one, but it still counted.

My mom came out on the porch as Freedom and I walked up.

"Mom, look! I'm riding a horse!" I yelled. Then I laughed right out loud.

"Guess I don't have to tell you to smile," the man said from behind the camera.

CLICK!

The photographer helped me down from Freedom's back, and I gave the pony a good-bye pat. Then I ran to get my green glass jar and counted out fifty pennies.

"You're going to have one humdinger of a picture!" the man told me.

A Note from the Author

Life was a lot different for kids growing up during the years 1939 to 1945. They didn't have electronic games. If they wanted to play inside, they played checkers or Monopoly. They didn't have frozen pizza. If they wanted a snack, their moms made popcorn by rattling and shaking a kettle on the top of the stove. And they didn't have television, either. Families gathered around the radio in the evening to listen to shows like *Fibber McGee and Molly* or *The Lone Ranger.* Everyone was eager to hear the war news, because this was the time of World War II.

The author in 1942

While many went off to war, those on the home front did what they could to help the war effort. If a family member was fighting overseas, a service flag with a blue star hung in the front window of the home. The families of service people killed in action displayed flags with gold stars.

The war changed the way people lived, worked, ate, and played.

There were food shortages. The government gave each family rationing stamps, which allowed them to buy only a certain amount of sugar, butter, meat, and other foods each week. In spite of the scarcity of food, though, many mothers saved bacon fat, lard, and other cooking fats.

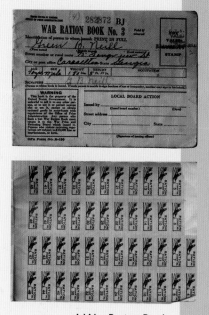

A War Ration Book and stamps

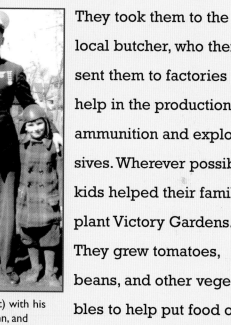

The illustrator (left) with his older brother, Donn, and younger brother, Mark, in 1945

They took them to the local butcher, who then sent them to factories to help in the production of ammunition and explosives. Wherever possible, kids helped their families plant Victory Gardens. They grew tomatoes, beans, and other vegetables to help put food on the dinner table. Treats like bubble gum, candy, or anything made with sugar were rare.

Things made from rubber were also hard to get, even rubber bands for ponytails.

Rubber was needed to make tires for war vehicles. Many shoes had rubber soles and heels, so even shoes were rationed. Kids often had only one pair. When children wore holes through the bottom of their shoes, their mothers cut cardboard linings to fit inside them. Kids had to be careful not to step in rain puddles!

There was also a shortage of paper goods. Paper was needed for cartons to ship war supplies overseas, so mothers took cloth bags to the stores to carry groceries home. People sneezed into handkerchiefs rather than paper tissues. Schools held paper drives. It wasn't unusual to see a kid walking to school pulling a red wagon stacked with newspapers he'd collected from his neighbors. Kids were sometimes called papertroopers.

Children collect old bed frames and other metal items.

Anything made with metal was in short supply. Families rummaged through basements and attics, looking for metal items they could do without: baby buggy frames, old pots and pans, even tin bread boxes. They rinsed and flattened tin cans to be collected. People saved empty metal toothpaste tubes and returned them to the drugstore when they bought a new tube. Kids did their part by gathering up any toys made from metal (there were no plastic toys yet): trucks, trains, dollhouses, tea sets. All of these metal items were sent to factories to be turned into airplanes and tanks.

Automobile manufacturers stopped making cars. Even a family lucky enough to own one couldn't do much driving, because gasoline was rationed and only a limited amount was allowed each week. Because of this, horses were used to pull the many trade wagons up and down city streets.

The war years were difficult, but families and communities worked together to help each other and their country. Kids were an important part of that community. They worked hard. They played hard. On any summer day, the calls of "red rover, red rover" or "ollie-ollie-oxen-free" could be heard, mixed with the jangle of harnesses and the clopping of the street horses as they made their way through the neighborhoods.

PLANT A VICTORY GARDEN

OUR FOOD IS FIGHTING

A GARDEN WILL MAKE YOUR RATIONS GO FURTHER

Government posters encouraged citizens to support the home front war effort.

In loving memory of my dad, Paul Kozak
–D. C.

For my brother, Donn
– T. L.

Ω

Published by
PEACHTREE PUBLISHERS
1700 Chattahoochee Avenue
Atlanta, Georgia 30318-2112
www.peachtree-online.com

Text © 2007 by Dori Chaconas
Illustrations © 2007 by Ted Lewin

Book and jacket design by Loraine M. Joyner

Illustrations created in watercolor on 100% rag archival
watercolor paper; text typeset in Monotype Corporation's
Rockwell; title type designed with International Typeface
Corporation's Novarese.

Printed in Singapore

10 9 8 7 6 5 4 3 2 1
First Edition

Library of Congress Cataloging-in-Publication Data

Chaconas, Dori, 1938-
    Pennies in a jar / written by Dori Chaconas ; illustrated by
Ted Lewin. -- 1st ed.
        p. cm.
    Summary: A young boy whose father is serving overseas
during World War II struggles to overcome his fears, especially his fear of the horses that pull trade wagons through his
neighborhood, as he works odd jobs for money to buy his
father a birthday present.
    ISBN 13: 978-1-56145-422-8
    ISBN 10: 1-56145-422-2
    [1. Horses--Fiction. 2. Fear--Fiction. 3. Fathers and sons--
Fiction. 4. Peddlers and peddling--Fiction. 5. World War, 1939-
1945--Fiction. 6. United States--History--1939-1945--Fiction.] I.
Lewin, Ted, ill. II. Title.
    PZ7.C342Str 2007
    [E]--dc22
                                        2006103227

Photo credits: author photo on page 34 courtesy of Dori
Chaconas. Illustrator photo on page 34 courtesy of Ted Lewin.
Ration book and stamps on page 34 courtesy of J. P. Rowe. Scrap
metal drive photo on page 35 courtesy of Library Congress Prints
and Photographs Division (LC-USF34-072477-D). Victory garden
photo on page 35 courtesy of U. S. Office of War Information (poster
no. 34, 1943).